THE
BattlestaR
GALACTICA
STORYBOOK

THE

BattlestaR
GALACTICA

STORYBOOK

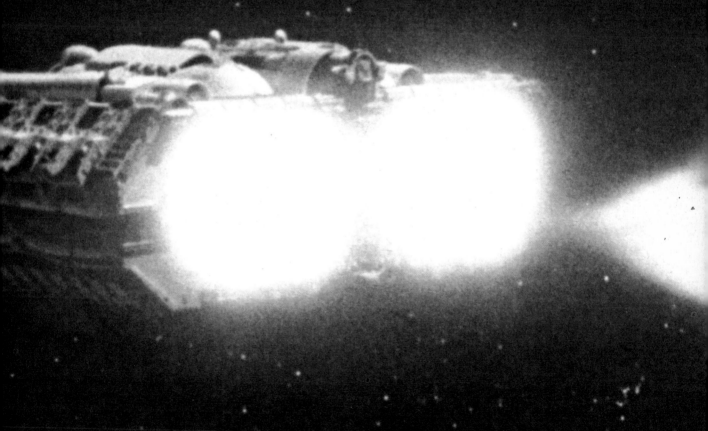

SCHOLASTIC BOOK SERVICES

NEW YORK · TORONTO · LONDON · AUCKLAND · SYDNEY · TOKYO

Based on the film by Glen A. Larson
and the novel by Glen A. Larson and Robert Thurston
Story adapted by Charles Mercer
Book Design by Kathleen Westray

ISBN 0-590-30091-1

12 11 10 9 8 7 6 5 4 3 2 1   1   0 1 2 3 4 5/8

Printed in the U.S.A.

Boomer—A brave fleet warrior, based on *Galactica*

Adama—Commander of the mighty battlestar *Galactica*, the greatest ship in the Colonial Fleet

Apollo and **Starbuck**—Adama's son, a Viper fighter captain, and his friend, a bold fighter pilot

Boxey and **Muffit Two**—An orphan from Caprica with his amazing mechanical daggit, Muffit Two

Athena—Adama's daughter, an ensign on the battlestar

Cassiopeia—Beautiful refugee from Caprica, captured by the Ovions on Carillon

Serina—Newswoman from Caprica who rescues Boxey

Imperious Leader—Brilliant, evil Cylon Commander, determined to destroy mankind, and a Cylon

Young Zac's father, Commander Adama, had warned him not to get too excited about the war. After all, it had been going on for a thousand years—no need to welcome it as your best friend. But Lieutenant Zac never lost the thrill of zooming through space in his sleek fighter and blasting Cylon craft to bits.

Now, on advance patrol for the Colonial Fleet, Zac saw on his scanner two unidentified aerial devices hanging near an old moon. The voice of his older brother, Captain Apollo, came from a fighter scouting a distance away: "Better have a look. Kick in the turbos."

"But Apollo," Zac replied on the intercom, "the standing orders on conserving fuel specifically forbid use of turbos."

"Zac," Apollo said, "don't let the coming peace conference interfere with your judgment. Till we get official notice of a signing, anything goes. These are still the front lines."

In an instant they were over their objective. It was a big, old vehicle, floating aimlessly in the sea of space. Below it stretched a layer of purple clouds.

"What is it?" Apollo whispered.

Zac punched out the combination that would identify the picture on the scanner. "Warbook says an old Cylon tanker," he reported. "Scanner reads it empty."

"Well, kid," Apollo said, "we came to look. Let's get up closer."

Zac watched Apollo's Viper peel off. Then he set his own flight pattern to follow, hitting the course buttons sharply. When they broke through the cloud layer, Zac let out a gasp. They had flown smack into a huge Cylon staging area.

As far as they could see there were Cylon warships, with their odd curves and arclike limbs. In one of the ships Apollo saw the usual trio who composed a Cylon fighting crew. Their tubular-shaped helmets covered many-eyed creatures with heads that apparently could change shape at will. In the center of the helmet was a long, narrow opening from which came concentrated beams of light. No human had ever discovered if the light was created by the Cylons themselves or was a part of the helmet. Suddenly, Apollo was startled to see one of the helmet lights swing upward toward his Viper. He punched a reverse loop on his directional touch plate. His ship, rolling upward and over, screamed off in a tight turn.

"Let's get out of here!" Apollo yelled.

Zac's Viper promptly rolled over and followed his brother's speeding craft. "Apollo!" His voice came shrilly on the intercom. "Cylon ships coming at me—firing!"

On his scanner Apollo made out four ships chasing his kid brother. He and Zac turned and attacked them. *Zap! Zap! Zap!* Three were destroyed in bright flashes of fire. But then a fresh wave of fighters came at them, and Zac lost an engine in the new attack.

"Go on!" he cried to Apollo. "I'll make it. You've got to get back and warn the Fleet. Go!"

Commander Adama was glad to get away from the spacecraft *Atlantia* on which the politicians were traveling to peace talks with the Cylons. Adama thought those politicians from the Twelve Colonies were being taken in. He was certain that the Cylons did not truly want peace. They were trying to lull the humans with an armistice—then destroy them.

When the shuttle set Adama down on the great fighting ·battlestar *Galactica*, which he commanded, he was glad to find his daughter, Athena, on the bridge. She was a beauty who reminded him of her mother—his wife, Ila, now home on Caprica. No wonder Starbuck and other officers vied for Athena's attention.

"Something's wrong," Ensign Athena told Adama.

His aide, Colonel Tigh, veteran of many battles with him, was squinting at his scanners intently. "A patrol in trouble. Their messages are being jammed. Has to be Cylons."

Adama **contacted** President Adar on the *Atlantia* by codebox and after explaining the situation said, "As a precautionary measure I'd like to launch intercept fighters." Behind Adar on the monitor came the skulking figure of Baltar, the trader who had led the politicians into peace talks with the evil Cylons. Baltar whispered in Adar's ear. Why did the President ever listen to him?

"Commander—" Adar spoke hesitantly after Baltar stopped whispering to him—"we could jeopardize the entire cause of peace by displaying fighters when we're so close to a meeting point with the Cylons."

Why couldn't the politicians see that the meeting with the Cylons for peace talks might be only a Cylon trap to destroy the entire Home Fleet?

"Mr. President," Adama pleaded, "please at least put the Fleet on a state of alert."

"I'll consider it." The screen went blank.

"Commander!" Tigh turned to him sharply. "That patrol of Captain Apollo's—there are just two of them, he and Lieutenant Zac—they're under enemy fire. Their reports are being jammed. Can't we launch and go to their aid?"

"No. We're expressly forbidden to launch. But this is a good time to order a test of our battle stations drill."

The alert-horn blared loudly through the ready room where Starbuck was playing cards with two Gemons. Starbuck, knowing he had them beaten, had just said, "Okay, one hand. Sudden death." Next moment, someone racing to his battle station stumbled and knocked the winning cards from his hand.

Grumbling, Starbuck sprinted to his ship where Jenny, his ground crew chief warrant officer, closed the form-fitting cockpit over him. He taxied to his launch point where his craft joined the vast array of *Galactica*'s gleaming vehicles.

On the bridge, meantime, Tigh told Adama, "Starboard landing deck is ready for approaching single fighter." Then the watch officer said, "Sir, the long-range scanner picks up a large number of craft coming our way at high speed."

Adama tried vainly to figure some reason other than attack for the huge wall of ships closing in on them. Getting the President on the codebox again, he told him what was happening. Once more Baltar's puffy face appeared beside Adar's, and Adama demanded, "Are you going to allow our forces to sit here totally defenseless—"

"Commander!" The President spoke sharply. "We're on a peace mission. The first peace mission humans have known after a thousand years of war. What you see on your screen is probably a welcoming committee."

Tigh touched Adama's shoulder and said, "A lone ship of ours is under attack from the main approaching force."

Enraged, Adama shouted, "Hear that, Mr. President? That *welcoming* committee is firing on our patrol!"

Adar backed from the camera, his face and body seeming to collapse inward. "Baltar—Baltar!" he babbled. But the traitor Baltar had disappeared. "Commander Adama!" The President could think of nothing to say.

Adama whirled to the screen which showed Zac's Viper under attack. And then his young son's voice rang out joyfully: "See you now, *Galactica*! My scanner's working again. All's A-Okay!"

Suddenly, four Cylon ships closed on his, firing at the same time. Zac's craft exploded, became a flash of light, disappeared.

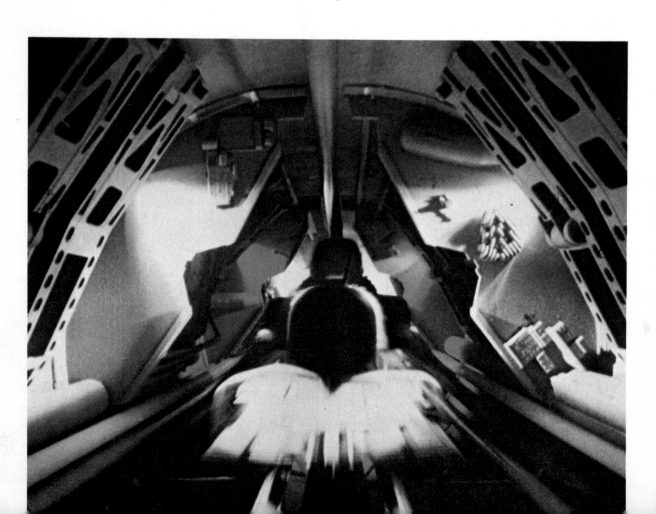

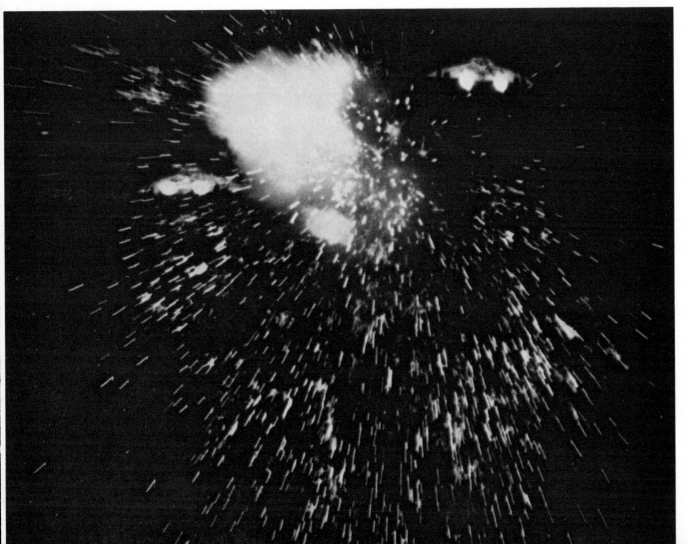

The Cylon commander, whose name would translate into human language as "Imperious Leader," sat above his officers on a huge pedestal. On his many-eyed, knobby head, he was wearing a helmet that was the Cylon version of the massive communications panel aboard *Galactica*. With it Imperious Leader kept track of all phases of the battle at the same time. In his third brain, the one that monitored the functioning of his lesser two brains, he enjoyed deep satisfaction. His entire life had been pointed toward this moment, the final and overwhelming defeat of the human pest that had infected the perfect unity of the universe.

Through the dead silence of the bridge President Adar's voice spluttered from the codebox: "Wh-wh-what was that!"

"That was *my son dying*, Mr. President," Adama's voice came sadly, bitterly. Then he turned and cried, "Launch fighters! All batteries commence firing!"

Now Imperious Leader's base ship approached the main target, the most important of the twelve human planetary targets to which he was leading the huge forces under his command. He personally would supervise the destruction of the planet Caprica. His spy network had informed him it was the home planet of his chief human enemy, Adama, and he

wanted the pleasure of its destruction himself. There were many things wrong with humans from the Cylon viewpoint. They were concerned about things like good and evil, which did not even exist to Cylons. This concern interfered with the Cylons' determination to preserve the natural order of the universe as they saw it. Humans' venturesome ways and wish to explore areas that were none of their business made it essential that Cylons wipe them out.

Imperious Leader saw that Adama, more than any other human he ever had studied, personified these evils of mankind.

Now an officer approached Imperious Leader's pedestal, and he gave him permission to speak. "All base ships are now in range to attack the Twelve Colonies."

Imperious Leader's many eyes glowed with elation. "Ah, the final annihilation of the alien pest, the life form known as man! Let the attack begin!"

No other Colonial Fleet battlestar besides *Galactica* was able to launch full forces of fighting craft in time. *Galactica*'s fighters, vastly outnumbered, dodged and flew at Cylon ships. Laser cannons fired and cross-fired, their bright, thin lines exploding into spectacular red and yellow flames when they found a target.

After Apollo landed safely from his scouting mission, he rushed to the bridge. Heartbroken over Zac's death, he felt he was somehow responsible. Adama and Athena, as saddened as he, tried to assure him it was no way his fault. But they had little time to say much to one another in the heat of battle.

Suddenly, Adama saw that there were no base ships in the attacking Cylon force, only fighters. The Cylon base ships must be on the way to attack the home planets! This fight was hopeless, but *Galactica* might yet save Caprica from destruction. He contacted the President, who looked badly frightened on the monitor. The *Atlantia* had been heavily hit. Fires blazed behind President Adar.

"Mr. President," Adama said, "I request permission to leave the Fleet."

"Leave the Fleet!" Adar screamed. "That's a cowardly—"

Before Adama could fully explain, a mighty explosion rocked the *Atlantia*. With a burst of blinding light, it blew apart and into a million pieces. All aboard *Galactica* watched in stunned silence. Tigh was the first to recover; he touched Adama's arm. "Look, our long-range scanners have picked up Cylon base ships here, here, and here. This puts them well within striking range of the planets Virgon, Sagittara, and— and—"

"I know." Adama suppressed a groan. "Caprica."

Athena set their course home to Caprica, where Adama had not returned on leave from active duty in two years.

———

Serina was the most famous newswoman on Caprica. She also was perhaps the most beautiful woman of any profession on the planet. Her auburn hair, green eyes, and slender, well-formed body had created a Caprican ideal of beauty. All of which sometimes bored Serina as she went about her daily routine of reporting news events.

The day it happened, Serina had just stepped in front of a television camera amid the all-glass buildings of the shopping mall in Caprica City when she heard a distant explosion. And then another—closer. Everyone in sight grew still. Suddenly a Cylon warship streaked low over the city, shooting bursts from laser weapons into the crowds. There was screaming everywhere as people fell, dead and wounded. The glass buildings popped like ancient electric light bulbs and great shards of falling glass fell on survivors who ran about in panic.

Serina, tearing off her microphone, dashed to help a small boy who was struggling from a pile of rubble and wailing frantically. She snatched him up, trying to comfort him. "Muffit!" he cried. "Where's my daggit, Muffit?"

Daggits, animals native to Caprica, had been easily domesticated by the first colonists. They were the favorite pet among younger children. Parents liked the four-legged, short-furred rascals because, in spite of their playfulness, they always protected children.

But Serina could not find Muffit or the boy's parents. She knew they must be dead in the debris. She tried to comfort the boy who was about six years old and had large brown eyes and brown hair. His name was Boxey. She had to try to get him and herself to safety, if there was any safe place left on the planet.

Adama, Athena and Apollo stared with horror at the scanner. The smoldering ruins of Caprica City filled the screen. Ila lived in the suburbs. *She has to be all right*, Athena told herself. Yet she knew that her mother must be dead. First Zac. Now this.

Her father's lean face was set grimly as he stared at the awful scene. What could Athena say to comfort him? Apollo cursed and began to pace the bridge, tears welling in his eyes. First Zac dead. Now Mother. What of comfort was left in life? Athena thought of Starbuck. She loved that handsome, crazy, gambling, daring pilot. But now he was gone too, probably never to return, along with his friend Boomer.

One of the hardest things about Adama's difficult decision to quit the hopeless battle had been that he had to leave most of his pilots in the air. Starbuck and Boomer were among the missing. Apollo had been angry with his father for deserting them. In vain Adama tried to explain that speed and secrecy were essential if *Galactica* were to go to the aid of Caprica. The pilots would find other landing and refueling spots and try to join the battlestar later. Apollo didn't buy that explanation.

For the time being *Galactica* was safe from Cylon observation in its camouflage force field as it hovered over the ruins of Caprica. But for how long?

Adama spoke to Tigh after a seeming eternity of silence. "What are the reports from the Twelve Worlds?"

"No hope, Commander."

"Prepare my shuttlecraft," Adama said. "I'm going down to the surface of Caprica."

Tigh was alarmed. "Sir, if the Cylon scanners pick you up when you get out of our camouflage force field, you won't have a chance."

"I am going," Adama said. "If I don't return, Tigh, proceed to a meeting with the survivors of the Fleet."

Apollo insisted on flying his father down to Caprica in his fighter. Athena wanted to go too, but Adama ordered her to remain on the *Galactica*.

When *Galactica* withdrew from battle, Starbuck almost fell out of his cockpit in anger. "What's going on?" he asked Boomer on the intercom.

"Don't ask me," Boomer replied. "Commander's calling the shots." There was an edge of sarcasm in Boomer's voice, the tone of the hardbitten pilot who knows you can't trust anybody in power.

"Heads up," Starbuck said. "You've got a pair on your tail." He flipped his craft over and took care of the two. His final thought about *Galactica* leaving the battle was, *There's got to be a good reason.*

But then he had no time to think about anything except the tough air battle. Several times he was nearly trapped in dreaded Cylon pinwheel attacks. In these, a dozen Cylon vehicles surrounded their target, and, in a complex series of sweeps, bore down on the human flyers. But he survived. And so did Boomer.

When their weapon supplies grew low and they could find no place to replenish them, he and Boomer took off in search of *Galactica*. Other fighters were doing the same. Starbuck and Boomer made it to one of the fueling stations hidden from Cylon view by camouflaging force fields. Fortunately, all were operating, so Starbuck, Boomer and many other fighters were able to go on till they could pick up the guidance system which led them to *Galactica*, hovering over Caprica.

Starbuck was almost out of fuel as he approached the big battlestar. Athena herself guided him in. As his ship shuddered into the entry port and hit the emergency force cushion, Starbuck blacked out.

When he came to, Athena was kissing him. "If this is a dream," Starbuck said, "I'm going back to sleep. Did Boomer make it?"

He had, and then Athena told him what had happened. Starbuck was sorry he ever had doubted Commander Adama.

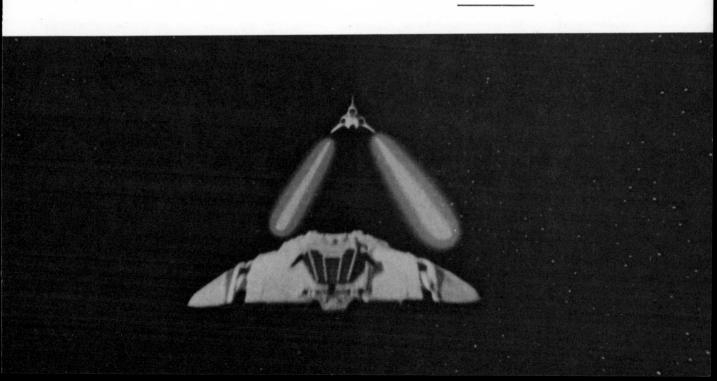

Adama, having made it safely with Apollo to the surface of Caprica, stood on the old familiar hill where his and Ila's house had been. The house was gone—and Ila with it. A battle scar ran in a deep rut across his land to the edge of the city where fires still raged. Adama was so shaken that he did not realize Apollo was following him.

Adama broke down and began to cry. "I'm sorry, Ila," he sobbed. "I never was here when it mattered. I was always away out there somewhere thinking that's where my duty was." He became aware of Apollo close behind him.

Apollo had seen his father break down. Sadly he turned and walked toward the spot where he had landed his fighter. When he reached the craft, a gang of angry, hysterical people was approaching. Ahead of them a beautiful young woman holding a little boy by the hand was trying to calm them. She was Serina, the little boy, Boxey.

"What about the Quorum of the Twelve?" she called to Apollo. "We're united, all we Twelve Worlds, after all these years. Surely we can fight back. Where are our leaders?"

Before Apollo could answer, his father spoke behind him. "Most of the leaders are dead. But yes, we can fight back."

Serina, recognizing him, cried, "Commander Adama!"

"But we can't fight back here or now," Adama told Serina and the crowd. "Not in the colonies, not even in this star system. We must gather together every survivor from each of the Twelve Worlds, every man, woman and child. We must get word to them to set sail at once in any vehicle that'll carry them, no matter what its state."

"Father," Apollo turned to him, "there isn't time to arrange provisions. The Cylons will be sending in landing parties to wipe out the survivors. We should send in our remaining fighters and—"

"No!" Adama said. "Too many of them, too few of us. There's a time to fight, but not now. We must withdraw and fight another day."

"But, Father, there's no way to board the entire population on the *Galactica*. We have no troop carriers left."

"We'll use what we do have," Adama said. "Every intercolony passenger liner, freighter, tanker, even intracolony buses, air taxis, anything that'll carry our people into the stars."

"And when they've gathered in the stars?" Serina asked him.

"We will lead them," Adama said, eyes glowing confidently. "And protect them till they're strong again."

Apollo imagined a ragtag fleet of all manner of ships rising from planets in flames. The survivors of all the colonies—the Aeries from Aeriana, the Gemons from Gemini, the Virgos from Virgon, the Scorpios, the Leos, the Picons, the Sagittarians. It didn't seem possible. But the determination on his father's face made him believe it was.

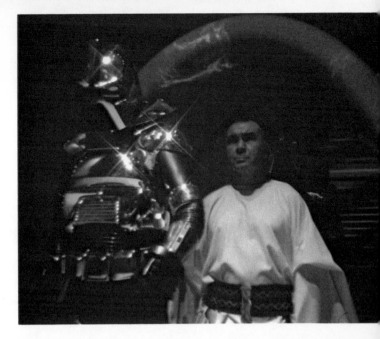

The Cylon Imperious Leader hated the sight of all humans. But none was more repulsive to him than this traitor, Baltar, who now stood before him. Traitors were the vilest of a vile race because they deliberately disturbed order for their own selfish gain.

"What of our bargain?" Baltar cried. "My colony was to be spared."

"The bargain was altered," Imperious Leader said. "Thanks for your help, Baltar. But you are no longer needed. Centurions!" Two appeared and took Baltar by either arm. "Take this human away," Imperious Leader said. "I have more important things to contemplate."

Baltar was dragged off, screaming.

Imperious Leader felt pleased. He was close to his goal now. Soon all humans would be destroyed and order restored to the universe.

Adama realized that the assembling of the survivors from the holocaust was a miracle. Not everyone made it. Indeed there was no way of knowing how many failed. But somehow many made their ways to the designated assembly point. Cylon search patrols passed near them, but they were not discovered.

Many of the survivor ships were old, frail space vehicles, but more slipped through the Cylon lines than Adama had expected. Almost twenty-two thousand ships of every colony, color, and creed of the Twelve Worlds were dredged up for use. Most were not suited to combat, but at least they were spaceships. They gave the human race, a small fraction of the population that had lived in the Twelve Worlds, another chance. A chance to survive—a chance to defeat the Cylons.

"But where are we going?" Athena asked her father.

When Adama finally gave his answer, all of those who mattered most to him—Athena, Apollo, Starbuck, Boomer, Tigh, Serina, Boxey—were present to hear him say: "Our parent race left their home on the planet Kobal and set out to establish colonies throughout the universe. It's all in the secret history books. Have any of you been privileged to read them?"

They had not.

"Well," Adama went on, "many planets were settled. But, because of dangers and disasters that wiped out many colonies, very few were successful. At last the Twelve Worlds were discovered. Exploration showed they were most habitable. So the remnants of all the other colonies were moved there. You know how they have thrived. But now we in this collection of ships are all who are left. We represent every known surviving colony, except one—"

"Except one?" Athena asked. "What do you mean, Father? Each of the Twelve Worlds has survivors and we're managing to rescue them."

"I'm not talking about the Twelve Worlds," Adama said. "I refer to a sister colony far out in the universe. Maybe it's not a colony. Maybe it did not succeed."

"All of us know something about that," Athena said. "It's been part of our mythology as long as any of us can remember. You mean a thirteenth colony, sometimes called Earth."

"That's right." Adama spoke slowly. "It's my intention to seek out that last remaining colony. Call it Earth or whatever. It may be the last outpost of humanity in the universe. Maybe it's a civilization like our own. Maybe its people are like us. We can ask their help in our rebuilding. Maybe we can warn them of the Cylons—the Alliance, as those creatures like to call themselves. It's the only solution we have. And we can be sure of one thing. The Alliance of Cylons will chase us across the universe."

"Sir," Starbuck said, "about this mythological colony—I don't think anybody even knows where it is. If we're going there, where are we to get the fuel and provisions?"

Tigh shook his head. "Commander, this isn't a fleet of sturdy, well-equipped soldiers up to battling the universe. Most of these people barely got away with their lives. They're physically and emotionally unprepared for the type of journey you propose."

Apollo spoke too. "Sir, less than half of these ships can make light-speed. It'll take us generations to find Earth."

"There is no choice," Adama replied measuredly. "If we mark time in this corner of the universe the Alliance will find us and wipe us out. No, we'll travel only as fast as our slowest ship. We'll be only as strong as our weakest brother or sister. I think there is a real world called Earth. I believe it's out there and will welcome us. We're going to try to find it."

———

Starbuck and Boomer, as all Fleet warriors, didn't like the lousy work details they had to perform. Crawling around old sky buses looking for fuel leaks was not their idea of fun. They entered a crowded, bad-smelling passenger compartment. The room was packed with people—old, young, crippled, babies in arms—lying on the floor and jammed against packing cases.

"Where is the food?" shrieked a bedraggled woman. An old man cried, "We haven't had water in two days!" Food—water. The cries were taken up everywhere in the compartment. An old couple on the floor appeared near death. A young woman tried to comfort them. Her own arm was badly mangled and broken.

Starbuck and Boomer approached to help them. But they were obviously frightened by the two warriors.

"What is your name?" Starbuck asked the young woman. "Cassiopeia," she replied. "Cassiopeia," Starbuck said, "will you help me reassure these people? We want to get them to a hospital ship. And your arm needs attention."

Cassiopeia spoke to the couple and they let Starbuck and Boomer carry them out. They were just in time, for the angry crowd started closing in on them. "Oh no!" Boomer muttered as he locked the hatch. Starbuck called for a shuttle to take the three passengers to emergency and said, "Those people are desperate. They're as dangerous as Cylons."

While Starbuck was flying the ill to a hospital ship, Apollo took Boomer with him on an inspection of food that was contaminated. As they came around a corner, Apollo bumped into Serina, who asked him to take a look at Boxey. "He's so depressed, Captain, I'm afraid he

might die. His parents are gone and he can't believe that his daggit is dead." Apollo started to say he was too busy, but Serina was so upset that he followed her.

Boxey lay in a curtained-off niche staring at the ceiling. "I want Muffit," was all he would say at first. But after Apollo talked to him and pinned one of his officer's bars on the child's tunic, Boxey began to feel better. "He's going to get the first daggit that comes along," Apollo told Serina. She suddenly liked this Captain Apollo—especially when he stopped acting like a warrior and took time to comfort a child.

Serina had not used her connections as an influential newswoman to get Boxey and herself comfortable living quarters in the elite section of this former luxury space liner called *Rising Star.* Apollo was impressed by that as he and Boomer went on toward the elite class on inspection.

"This is disgusting," Boomer said after they entered the area. It was disgusting indeed. While people were starving in some other compartments, here in elite class all was luxury. The wealthy, who apparently had bought their way in, were eating and drinking greedily. The grand ballroom had been turned into a kind of throne room and there one Sire Uri reigned like a king. Uri had been hated by honest folk throughout the Twelve Worlds for his corrupt ways in politics. In escaping to this spaceship *Rising Star* he and his friends had looted museums of all of value they could bring with them. Now paintings and sculptures crowded the walls of the ballroom so that it looked like a huge art gallery. These friends who had come into elite class with Uri had elected him a member of the new Fleet Council.

Now Councilman Uri reacted with anger when Apollo and Boomer burst into his party in the ballroom. He was furious when Apollo told Boomer, "Notify Core Command that we've located some new food stores and will distribute them to the needy as far as they'll go." When Uri threatened him, Apollo said, "You're under arrest, Uri. The charge is hoarding food. It was agreed everything would be distributed fairly." Uri turned red with rage as two guards led him away.

"Captain," Boomer said, "without being critical, are you sure you didn't overplay your hand? Remember, Sire Uri is on the new Council and could be a dangerous enemy."

"He doesn't worry me," Apollo said. "And as for overplaying my hand, this isn't one of your and Starbuck's card games, Boomer. Those people down below are starving. They've got to be fed."

"I know," Boomer said. "I'm on your side."

Sire Uri had been causing trouble for Adama ever since his election to the Council. His being arrested didn't help matters after friends quickly arranged his release. Uri never stopped criticizing Adama. The Commander knew there were times when a leader had to act like a tyrant in order that his followers would do necessary things. But he did not enjoy having to act like one.

At last Adama decided to resign command of the expedition and let the Council run things for a while. Old friends and followers begged him not to resign, but he felt it was for the best that he do so. He had another hard decision to make—one he knew would be unpopular when he presented it to the Council: "The problem is that there are too many of us. Too many people, too many ships. We would have had troubles even if so much of our food supplies had not been contaminated. Even if so many of our ships had not proved to be in such poor condition. We *must* obtain food and fuel. That's our only solution. Otherwise, we all perish— slowly and gradually, as our supplies run out. We have to convert all the ships we can to greater capabilities. Those ships we can't convert we'll have to leave."

"That just means more overcrowding,"

Uri complained.

"True, Uri. That's why I propose we pool our stock of fuel and send *Galactica* and our better fighting ships ahead. They'll get supplies for the rest of us."

"Leave ships behind?" shouted Uri. "Let them be destroyed by the warships of the Alliance?"

"They should be perfectly safe," Adama said. "Our long-range patrols say their scanners show no sign of pursuit by the Cylons. The camouflage shielding that Apollo devised is holding steady. Except for one flyby a while ago no Cylon flight team has come anywhere near us."

But where, a Councilwoman asked, did Adama propose that the advance guard go in search of fuel and food?

"Carillon," Adama said. "That planet was once the object of a mining expedition from the Twelve Worlds. There are rich sources of Tylium there." Tylium was what fueled their spaceships.

"But," Uri said, "Carillon was abandoned because it wasn't practical to mine the Tylium."

"It was abandoned," Adama replied, "only because there was no local labor and it was too far from the Twelve Worlds to make shipping practical."

The Councilmen and Councilwomen

argued for a long time. A unanimous vote was necessary for such a vital move. At last Uri was the only holdout against Carillon. He finally was made to agree when Adama said his ship *Rising Star* could go ahead with the advance expedition. Uri was afraid of being left behind.

———

After the Council meeting, which Apollo and Serina attended as interested spectators, he asked her how Boxey was doing.

"Not well," she said. "He doesn't want to eat, can't sleep."

"Maybe I have a cure," Apollo said. "Let's pick up Boxey and go to a place I have in mind." Both she and Boxey followed him to a door on a lower level of *Galactica* lettered Droid Maintenance Laboratory.

"Droids," Serina said dubiously, and Boxey asked, "What's a droid?" Apollo explained they were mechanical toys which looked and acted like animals or humans, depending on what you wanted the toy to do.

When they went into the laboratory the chief technician said, "We've been expecting you, Captain Apollo. Is this the young officer who's been put in charge of the new project?" Apollo nodded while Boxey looked up at the technician wide-eyed. "We'll soon be landing on strange new planets," the technician told Boxey. "Ordinarily we'd have daggits to guard our people while they sleep. But we weren't able to bring any live ones with us. So we've had to design a mechanical one—a droid. We've named him Muffit Two. See here."

Of course Boxey knew that this Muffit Two was not a real daggit, but something made of wires and fur and mechanical parts. But he looked completely real when the technician put him on the floor. Barking and wagging his tail in friendly fashion, he came to Boxey. The boy crouched down, staring at him. Then Muffit Two rose on hind legs, and Boxey gathered him into his arms. For the first time since Serina and Apollo had known him, Boxey was smiling.

"Thanks, Doc," Apollo told the technician. "That's one I owe you."

"Any time," the technician said.

As they followed Boxey and his new pet into the corridor, Serina said to Apollo, "And that's one I owe you."

"Any time," he replied, smiling.

She smiled too. "You look smug, but I'm going to kiss you anyway."

———

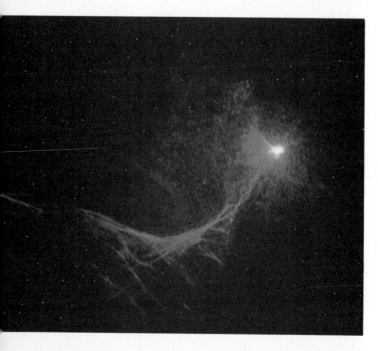

Adama grew tense as *Galactica* and the few other ships able to make the jump through hyperspace arrived in the sector containing the planet Carillon. If they could not obtain a good supply of Tylium here, the entire expedition was doomed to destruction.

Almost as soon as they had materialized in Carillon's solar system, the bridge scanner announced an obstacle on which they had not planned. The Commander called up his three best pilots—Boomer, Starbuck, and Apollo—to brief them on their unexpected mission.

"It appears," he told them, "the skies around Carillon are heavily mined."

"Who," asked Apollo, "would bother to do that at an obscure place like this?"

"For the moment, Captain, that's irrelevant," his father replied. "The point is the mines prevent us from getting into a position to take on supplies. We have to find a path in. No time for elaborate searches. You'll have to navigate by scanner and sweep everything out of your path with turbolasers. Any questions?"

"Yes sir," Starbuck said. "Would this be a good time for me to take my sick leave?"

"Yes." Adama smiled. "But permission denied. One thing I notice about this minefield. Every mined satellite is firmly in orbit. No sign of a decaying orbit anywhere. The implication is strong that the minefield is maintained on a regular basis, so there has to be somebody down there on Carillon's surface."

"And it's a good chance they're mining Tylium?" Apollo asked.

"Right. They've got to be doing something sinister to bother with all this protection."

Athena was distraught that her father had ordered both Starbuck and Apollo on this new, dangerous mission. Adama knew that she loved Starbuck. They

talked together about her wish for a hus-
band, children, a home. Such things sim-
ply would have to wait. Athena under-
stood that, but talking about it with her
father made her feel better.

At launch time Starbuck knew he was
starting on his most dangerous mission
ever. The scanners showed three kinds of
mine in this field they had to penetrate.
One was the normal explosive type. A
second seemed more instrument than
weapon, with electronic equipment all
over its surfaces. The third type offered
the most trouble: instead of exploding, it
sent off flashes of light so intense that it
would blind anyone who looked at it. Because of that danger, the pilots had to fly
their mission with cockpits darkened and
treated with a chemical to ward off the
ray.

The trouble with that, Starbuck grum-
bled to himself, was that they had to fly
blind against *all* the mines. After the
three pilots were launched, Apollo said
he was going in first to test. In a moment
he let out an agonized yell.

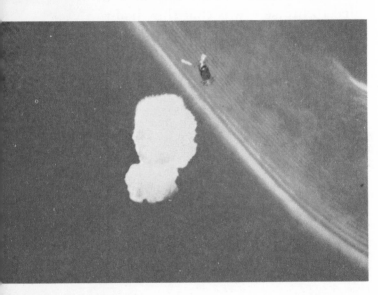

"What *is* it?" Starbuck shouted.

"Those mystery mines aren't mines at all. They're electronic jammers. Soon as I got near one, everything in this ship started going haywire. I was just able to pull out in time. Come in careful!"

On Starbuck's scanner one of the light mines was activated near the form of Apollo's fighter. "I'm okay," Apollo signalled, "but I'm veering off. Anybody make out anything else on their scanner about this field?"

"Negative," Starbuck said. "My scanner's burning up."

"Mine's gone," Boomer said.

"Only one thing I can think of, fellas," Apollo said. "Haul off, hold positions, and blast away."

"You mean run a path right through the minefield?" Starbuck said. "With our scanners out of whack and our cockpits dark?"

"Only way. Sound hard to you, Starbuck?"

"Nothing to it," Starbuck said sarcastically. "Easy as pie."

"What if we miss a mine?" Boomer said.

"One of us'll be the first to know it. Let's fly!"

On the *Galactica* bridge everyone was frozen by anxiety as the trio charged in. On the big screen they watched the ships angling through the minefield, the three pilots firing everything they had with stunning accuracy. Mine after mine exploded and disappeared. Suddenly, when it became clear that Apollo's daring plan was going to work, a cheer went up on the bridge.

It was echoed by Boomer's victory cry out in space: "Yaaahooo!"

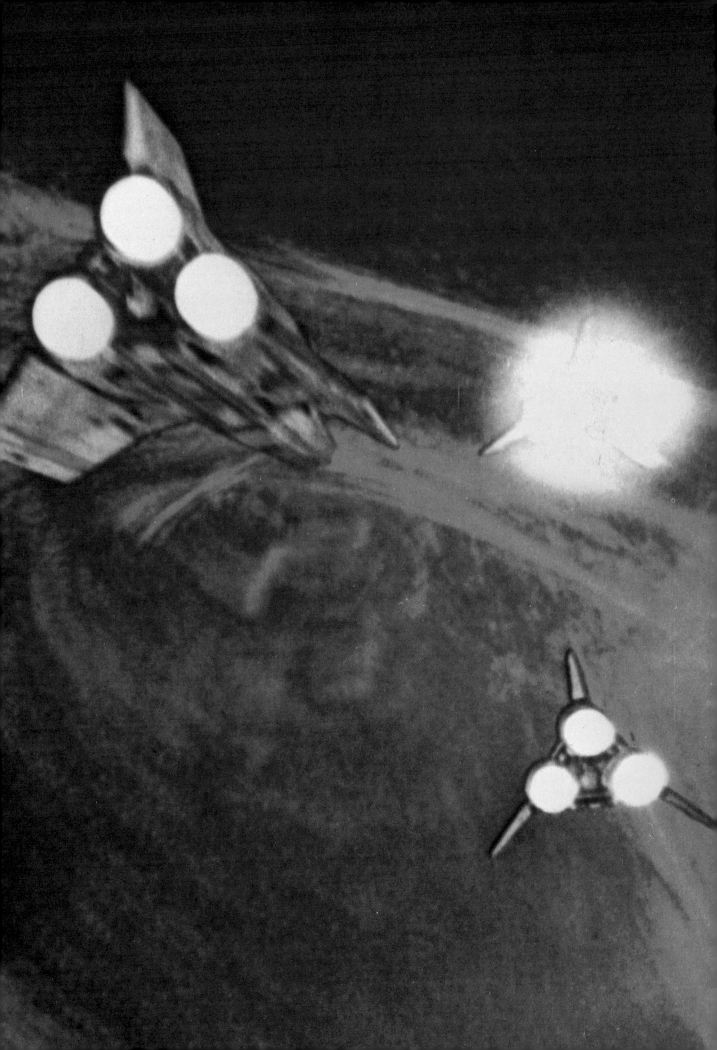

Imperious Leader thought about the minor failures in his generally successful plan of eliminating all humans from the universe. He knew there were a few ships left, but where were they? Cylon scouting ships could not find them.

Then a message came along the Cylon network. Some mines in the protective field around Carillon had been set off. But it was doubtful the humans had anything to do with that. More likely it was the work of space pirates who had heard rumors about the importance of the Tylium mining there. In all these years of war the humans never had discovered that Carillon was the prime source of fuel for their enemy. Well, Imperious Leader decided, a careful watch must be kept on events on the planet Carillon.

After the three pilots cleared the minefield protecting Carillon, the farming ships landed. They took quick advantage of the planet's fertile soil, which offered the chance of quick-growth foodstuffs. The farmer-technicians collected as much grazing material from the Carillon surface as they could and transplanted it to the special food spaceships from the Twelve Worlds.

Boomer and Starbuck were sent to the far side of the planet to explore mining possibilities. They reported it pleasant and quiet.

What neither they nor the main body of explorers realized was that while they were observing, they were being closely observed. The observers were Carillon insectoids. Each of these spies was about five feet tall, with large bulbous eyes near the top of oval heads, long thin trunks, and four arms, each of which was busy with either two-triggered weapons or multi-lensed cameras. One took aim at Starbuck, but was stopped from killing him.

Seetol, a leader of the race called the Ovions by the few humans unlucky enough to face them, had for the moment decided not to kill any of the invaders. At least not until she had reported to her queen. At a nod from Seetol, another Ovion opened an aperture in the ground under a rock and all the Ovions disappeared into it. Seetol followed underground passages to the throne room of Queen Lotay.

"They have come," Seetol said softly.

Queen Lotay shrugged, as best a creature of her dimensions could. A slave held a long tube to her, from which she occasionally inhaled and blew out something that would look like smoke to humans.

"Don't disturb them," the queen said. "It will only stir them up."

Meanwhile, Boomer and Starbuck came down a hillside in their explorations and happened onto a scene they found hard to believe. People were laughing in beautiful gardens surrounded by glassed buildings. They were humans! No one paid any attention as Starbuck and Boomer strolled in.

Suddenly a beautiful woman let out a scream and pointed at Starbuck. "Why," she demanded, "are you Colonial Warriors sneaking around a perfectly respectable resort with pistols drawn?"

Starbuck grinned at her. "Nothing personal. We were just chasing what we took to be a bunny-rabbit. How did you get here?"

The woman scowled at him. "On the bus. How else?" She walked away, and Boomer said, "Old buddy, she must've been sniffing plant vapors."

They wandered on into a huge gambling casino where every game of chance ever known anywhere was being played. "Oh wow, Boom-Boom," Starbuck said in wonder. "Farewell, Starbuck," Boomer replied.

They stared with amazement at all kinds of inhuman and humanoid life.

There were tentacled lizards, furry octopods, a grotesque sexpartite set of connected individuals from a species that the two men had heard of only in legend. There were bulky, hard-surfaced oddities that would be mistaken for rocks if they hadn't moved and talked—creatures of all varieties and shapes. However, most were humanoid, sometimes oddly so.

A human pit boss invited them to gamble. "No thanks," Boomer said, but Starbuck answered, "Well—" In an instant a simian waitress supplied him drink and food. With a Sagittarian straight-arrow cocktail in one hand and an Aquarian ambrosia cake in the other, Starbuck watched the roll of dice and made plans to lose a fortune he didn't possess. But he found himself winning as never in his life.

"There's something phony about this," Boomer said.

Starbuck looked at the mound of cubits he had won quickly and asked his friend, "You mean to tell me these aren't real?"

They moved on to the Hi-Lo table, where Boomer still refused to gamble. An attractive young woman looked at Starbuck and said, "Well, well, the fleet's in. Sit down, *Lieutenant*, and make your fortune. You've come to the luckiest table in town."

Some distance from the gambling casino, Apollo had brought Serina and Boxey in by air taxi for a look at Carillon. On the intercom he asked the exploration chief what had become of Starbuck. "Strange to report, sir," the chief replied, "we haven't heard from him and Boomer in hours. They're lost!"

"You can't *lose* somebody like Starbuck," Apollo said to Serina. "He's too noisy."

Suddenly the Tylium detector in their craft started beeping. Apollo slowed and checked the indicator. It displayed a Tylium lode, a large one. When he stopped the vehicle, Muffit leaped out a window. Boxey ran after him, saying, "I'll be right back."

"Keep an eye on Boxey," Apollo told Serina. "We still don't know much about what's on this planet."

She called to Boxey to come back, but he had disappeared over a low hill in pursuit of Muffit. "We'll go after him," Apollo said.

———————

Seetol emerged from her ground cover and quickly swept Boxey and Muffit into her four-armed grasp. Before Boxey could scream or Muffit bark, Seetol had carried them underground. Through underground passages she brought them to Queen Lotay's throne room. The queen never had seen anything as amusing as this human child and his daggit. She told Seetol she was going to keep them and anyone who came looking for them must be put out of the way.

Moments later, as Serina and Apollo searched for Boxey and Muffit, Serina cried out. Two Ovion warriors had come out of a hole in the ground and were aiming their weapons at them.

The two soldiers forced them down long corridors until they came out in the enormous main chamber of the mine. Apollo exclaimed, "Father was right about there being Tylium here. Enough just in sight here to fuel all our ships and run them half-way across the universe. But who uses all this energy—and for what?"

When they were brought before Queen Lotay, she was perched on a high pile of cushions and spoke in her shrill, scratchy voice: "Welcome to Carillon. I assume you are impressed."

"Outraged is the word," Apollo said. "Where is the boy Boxey?"

The queen did not answer, but led them into a chamber which began to move slowly. This entire room was an elevator! When it stopped, they stepped out into a large banquet hall. It was crowded with noisy people stuffing themselves from mounds of food while music played loudly.

Starbuck hurried toward them. "Apollo! Serina! What luck!"

"I'm not sure it is," Serina said.

"Starbuck!" Apollo sounded angry. "People are starving back on our ships and here you are stuffing yourself—"

"Ease off, Captain." Starbuck spoke through a full mouth. "Try some of the orange wine. Delicious! These people are collecting food for us right now. Our problems are solved."

The queen was smiling oddly. Apollo and Serina looked at her, then at each other. Their eyes exchanged the doubt that anything at all was solved.

At last the centurion sent secretly to Carillon sent a message to Imperious Leader, telling him that humans definitely had arrived in the Carillon sector. Some already had been taken in by the Cylons' Ovion allies. Others hovered in orbit around the planet aboard *Galactica* and other spaceships. Their fighters had destroyed large sections of the minefield with which the Cylons had encircled Carillon by treaty arrangement with the Ovions in order to protect the Tylium supplies. The Cylon centurion sent word to Imperious Leader that he had entrenched himself in an underground cavern and was ready for action.

Action there would be—and quickly, Imperious Leader announced. He ordered a large fleet of Alliance fighters on the planet Borallus put in readiness to fly to Carillon. Then he relaxed and awaited the destruction of the last humans left in the universe.

Adama, studying the image of the planet Carillon in a viewer aboard his battlestar, thought that all looked well down there. The ships were beginning to take on food and fuel. Livestock aboard the ships was being well fed and the first agricultural growths already had sprouted. Then Tigh came to him, looking troubled.

"It's Sire Uri again, Commander. Always messing things up when they're going well. What office is he running for now—Commander in Chief? Anyway, he's handing out passes to anybody who wants to go down to the surface for a look around. And just about everybody does want to go. And not in the work parties. They want to go for fun."

They were interrupted by Athena, who asked permission to go down to the surface. Adama grimaced and said, "You too? To have some fun, I suppose."

"Father, I want to go because of Starbuck. I'm worried about him. He's down there, supposedly arranging for the transport of supplies. But there's a gambling casino down there, and you know Starbuck and—"

"Oh go ahead," Adama told her, "and bring that crazy pilot back here with you." After she had gone, Adama said to Tigh, "Think I'll go down and see a bit of that paradise for myself."

"Commander, are you sure you want to—"

"Are you suggesting I get permission from Sire Uri?"

"No sir! I'll have your shuttle ready!"

Adama never had seen anything like the Tylium mine the Ovions operated on Carillon. The workers, though live beings, acted like machines. The guards watched them so closely that it looked like slave labor to Adama. The supply of Tylium in this mine must be the biggest anywhere in the universe. But the way living beings were made to work at it was inhuman. Adama did not like it.

After he had inspected the mine with Queen Lotay and she had taken him to the banquet hall, he did not like what he saw there either. Sire Uri, other Council members and many other visitors from the fleet were eating and drinking like pigs while Lotay and members of her court passed among them, saying, "Please do enjoy yourselves. Be our guests. Be well fed, entertained. Be content."

Suddenly Adama did not trust her any more than he ever had trusted Sire Uri. He could not bring himself to swallow a bite of food. Despondent, he sat down in a chair near the entrance. Soon he took the shuttle back to his battlestar.

———————

As Starbuck moved on to a new table in the casino, he spotted a familiar face. It was the young woman with the broken arm he had taken to the hospital ship. "Cassiopeia," he called. "You look wonderful. Your arm is all fixed!"

"Starbuck!" she smiled. "I'm glad to see you again. Yes, Dr. Payne was able to fuse the bone whole with one of his fantastic machines. I'm as good as new!"

"Great," Starbuck told her. "Come to the table with me and bring me luck."

They sat down at the table and Starbuck was off and running. He'd never seen anything like this winning streak.

"Yeehoooo!" he cried, as if he had shot down another enemy Cylon out in space. His huge pile of golden cubits got higher as he tossed another winning hand back into the center of the table. When Cassiopeia said she was leaving for a minute and would be right back, Starbuck scarcely paid attention. "Let 'em ride again!" he yelled to the dealer.

"This seat taken?" a woman asked.

Starbuck looked up at Athena. "Well . . . " He began to squirm.

"Starbuck, I owe you an apology," Athena said, sitting down in the empty chair beside him. "When I came here looking for you, Boomer told me you were sitting with a beautiful lady."

"Well . . . " Starbuck gave her a thin smile. "Now, I am, honey."

"Thanks, Starbuck. I haven't seen much of you lately. What have you been up to?"

"Busy," Starbuck muttered, studying his cards.

"Starbuck," Cassiopeia said, coming up behind them, "you didn't save my seat."

"Oh, Starbuck, is this a friend of yours?" Athena asked, looking annoyed.

But Starbuck was too busy betting on a new hand to answer either Athena or Cassiopeia.

"Well," Athena said. "It looks like he doesn't have time for either of us. Shall we both leave?"

"Yeehoooo!" cried Starbuck, raking in another pile of cubits. When he looked up, Athena and Cassiopeia were walking off together.

Next thing Boomer was tapping him on the shoulder and insisting they go into the adjoining lounge. "There's something phony about this whole place," Boomer whispered.

"Tell me something phony about all these golden cubits I just won," Starbuck said.

"That's what I mean," Boomer said. "You ever before been in a place where you can't lose your money?"

"I've never been *here* before," Starbuck said. "Wow, look at the beautiful girls."

They were a trio of humanoid female singers known as Tucanas because they were from the planet Tucan. Their music for the customers in the lounge was weird, but the weirdest thing about the singers was the fact each had two mouths.

"Stop looking at the girls and listen to me," Boomer said. "Have you picked up any important information around here?"

"I can't stop looking at 'em," Starbuck said. "Did you ever before see a girl with two mouths?"

"No," Boomer replied, "but one time I had a girl who did a lot of double-talk. Listen to me, Starbuck." But Starbuck would not listen, and Boomer threw up his hands in disgust. Was there something about the food or drink served in this place that was making everybody who consumed much of it act crazy?

Around that time the same thought occurred to Serina and Apollo. They had felt happy ever since Boxey had been restored to them. Queen Lotay had taken care of that soon after she had showed them the banquet hall. Boxey was vague about where he'd been. Just lost, they concluded, but the Ovions had found him again. Muffit Two was with him, of course, and Boxey was happy—but sleepy.

Serina and Apollo put him and Muffit in one of the many bedrooms in this hotel-like place which the Ovions offered their visitors. When they looked at him last, he was sound asleep in bed and Muffit was guarding him alertly.

Then they wandered into the casino garden where a throng of humans was gathered around the fountain. They were drinking something in golden goblets that crew members of the *Galactica* called grog. Urged to try some, they did, and found that it seemed to mix hot and cold in delicious bursts of taste. Uri was there, drinking goblet after goblet of grog and sounding off about the queen, whom he now was calling "Lorry or something. . . . She's very kind, generous, even attractive if you can adjust your thinking to one of these insect creatures. . . ."

Apollo and Serina agreed that Uri

sounded sillier than he ever had. But after they'd drunk some grog, Uri didn't sound as silly to them as he had at first. It was then that both vaguely wondered the same thing Boomer had: Was there something about the food or drink in this place that made you act crazy? But soon they didn't much care because they were enjoying acting crazy themselves. All they wanted to do was kiss each other. And after they kissed, all they wanted to do was kiss again.

Lotay and Seetol went toward the pedestal room. Lotay was telling her devoted servant how she had disliked giving up Boxey. "But it was necessary for a while," she said. "But just for a while. I'll have him back soon to keep forever."

When they entered the room Seetol was annoyed to see that the Cylon centurion sent by Imperious Leader was seated on the queen's throne. Worse, Lotay was afraid of him and curtsied humbly.

"Our leader appreciates your cooperation," the centurion told her. "He intends to destroy every human left in this sector of space. Except, of course, any useful to your people."

Lotay bowed her head and said, "We are pleased, centurion."

She would have been surprised to know how carefully Imperious Leader was laying his plans. He had heard from his centurion, of course, how she was drugging the food and drink the Ovions served the humans and thus swaying their minds to foolish decisions. If only she could get some of the drug to Adama!

Cylon scouts finally had found that part of the human fleet which Adama had left behind when he went on to Carillon. Malfunction of their camouflage had given their coordinates away. But Imperious Leader had decided to leave them alone for the time being and concentrate on the armada he was sending from Borallus to attack the weaker force at Carillon.

Adama had never heard such nonsense as Uri was talking to the Council. *Make peace with the Cylons after all that had happened?* The man must be out of his mind. And the Council members must be out of *their* minds. All of them had returned to *Galactica* for today's meeting, bleary-eyed after a night on Carillon. Now they listened to Uri like people hypnotized. When he said they should accept Queen Lotay's proposal to decorate all the human pilots with the highest Ovion military medal, the Council actually cheered him. What was the matter with those people? But there was nothing that Adama could do about whatever ailed them.

Apollo, Starbuck and Boomer were among the pilots who returned to the battlestar briefly to change into dress uniform for the decoration ceremony. That, of course, would be held in the Ovion capital. Serina and Boxey were waiting there to see the ceremony.

After Apollo landed on the battlestar, he asked his father, "You're not attending the ceremony?"

"Of course not!" Adama snapped. "What difference does another medal make? That ceremony is just another ploy of Uri's. He's talking up to everyone the idea we should give up fighting and stay here in this safe paradise of Carillon. But I'm not at all sure it's in the least safe. Mark my words, at the ceremony Uri will propose we give up our arms and make peace. And under the great emotion of the occasion those fools probably will agree with him."

Apollo was stunned. Of course his father was right. He begged him to speak out, but Adama said, "I'm retired, son. Except for commanding this ship and running some aspects of the operation, I

never want even to talk to another politician if I can avoid it."

Apollo took the shuttle down to Carillon, and Adama began urging Tigh and his officers still on board to hurry up the loading of precious supplies from the planet.

Apollo, Serina and Boxey were waiting for an elevator to take them to the ceremony when Apollo saw something odd. A man wearing the dress uniform of *Galactica* Blue Squadron scurried away from them. The uniform fit him badly, and Apollo did not remember having seen him before. "That's funny," he said to Serina. "Thought I knew every man in the squadron."

Something similar was happening to Starbuck and Boomer on their way to the casino ceremony. They saw three men wearing ill-fitting Blue Squadron uniforms whom they did not know. Starbuck started after them to find out who they were, but they disappeared into a down-going elevator. Then Starbuck met Apollo, Serina and Boxey. He told Apollo about the strangers.

While they were talking, Muffit jumped out of Boxey's arms and ran into the casino. Boxey chased him, and Serina went after Boxey. Before she could catch up, they had run behind a screen and out of sight. Serina raced behind the screen. There was no one there. Boxey and Muffit had disappeared.

On the morning of the ceremony Cassiopeia was looking for Starbuck. She was going along a deserted corridor when an Ovion interrupted her thoughts of him by seeming to step from a wall. The creature put one of her four hands over Cassiopeia's mouth to stifle her screams and dragged her into a hidden pod-elevator.

She was carried, struggling all the way, several levels underground to a huge, dark chamber. A gang of Ovions flung her on a big table. A large cover came down quickly from the ceiling and sealed off her escape. A dark, reddish gas was pumped in through a tube, and everything grew vague to her.

———

Most of the human visitors now had assembled for the award ceremony. They would be easy targets when the proper time came, Seetol knew. Others of her troops were kidnapping humans who wandered away from the main body and taking them underground. All was going according to plan. Yet for some reason Seetol felt uneasy.

The Cylon centurion in command on Carillon had, of course, sent word of these preparations to Imperious Leader, who was pleased. Now that *Galactica* and the other ships had only token crews as they hovered above Carillon, he ordered his Supreme Star Force out of its ambush. Adama's force now was so weak that Imperious Leader knew he could destroy it with a single fighter sweep. What a relief to get rid of the human pest. He had been fighting humans so long that he was beginning to think like them.

Apollo and Starbuck were still puzzling over the three strangers from Blue Squadron. Without waiting for Serina to come back from the casino, Apollo said to Starbuck, "Let's find out what's going on here."

They could find no trace of the three men on the guest levels. So they tinkered with the elevator panel wires and were able to make it descend to the lowest level, where guests were forbidden to go.

They came out into an underground corridor. Ahead there was a sound of Ovion voices and sharp barking. Then the pilots saw an Ovion slashing a knife at Muffit while Boxey backed away from the creature.

"Run, Boxey!" Apollo shouted, amazed to see the boy here.

Boxey ran toward him, and the Ovion whirled around. Starbuck took a step forward and sent a beam of laser fire through the alien, who fell to the ground. Apollo started to lead the way around a turn of the corridor, then drew back. "A crowd of Cylons collecting there," he said to Starbuck.

"How did they get here?"

"They must have their own ways of getting through the minefield."

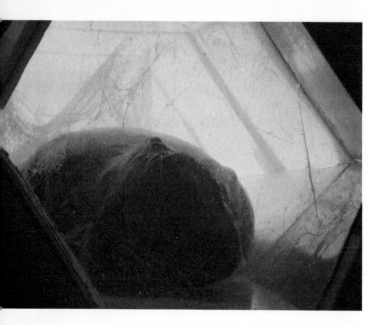

The Cylons had spotted them and started toward them. "Run!" Boxey led the way, and Apollo and Starbuck covered their flight with drawn sidearms. Before long they were hopelessly lost in the maze of passages. Then they found they were in a dead-end tunnel with the Cylons still pounding in pursuit behind them.

"Only one thing to do, old buddy," Apollo said. "Take them on shoulder to shoulder, blasting away with all we've got."

"Wait a second," Starbuck said. "What's the matter with that daggit?"

Muffit kept running away from them and back, barking frantically. "Follow him!" Boxey cried. "C'mon!" Muffit had found a small opening in a shadow of what appeared to be a blank wall. The two men, following Boxey, could barely squeeze through it. At last they came out into a large, shadowy cavern.

What appeared to be huge pods were growing on its floor. But when they took a closer look at one, they saw a human pinned under it. There was one under each pod, seeming to be only half-conscious. Starbuck swore and said that every one of these trapped humans had been gambling in the casino last night.

"We can't stay here now," Apollo said. "We'll send people back to release them. Right now there's the Cylons. Follow Muffit. He's the only one of us who seems to know where he's going."

They shrank down behind a pod as a group of Ovions entered the cavern carrying four new pods with humans in them.

"Oh no!" Starbuck cried. "That one there is Cassiopeia!" Before Apollo could stop him, he rushed at the Ovions. Boxey and Muffit ran after him despite Apollo's command to lie still. In an instant Starbuck was in the grip of two Ovion warriors. Queen Lotay, Seetol and a Cylon centurion appeared behind them.

"You can't turn her into—into *food!*" Starbuck shouted.

"Not precisely food, sir," Seetol said in her scratchy voice. "Although your nutrient substances are part of what is absorbed. They are diluted, in fact, into a liquid used to feed our babies when they hatch from the eggs."

Starbuck looked sick and said, "You're lower than a Cylon."

The Cylon centurion laughed harshly, and Seetol went on, "Within these pods, sir, we're able to extract all that's best in your race. And other races, for that matter. Minerals. Life-giving liquids. Bones for building materials. We can even extract knowledge from your brains, information from your body cells. You see, we use every bit of you usefully."

The queen, laughing too, reached out a tentacle and drew Boxey to her. Muffit let out a howl and sprang at her. But while the daggit was midway in the air, an Ovion warrior shot him down. He fell to the floor—no longer he, but *it*, a thing of wires and coils and false fur. Boxey let out a scream of rage and grief while the queen held him firmly.

Starbuck, swearing wrathfully, broke free of the eight-armed grasp of the two Ovion guards. Apollo, standing up, blasted a killing beam through the neck of the warrior who had destroyed Muffit. Starbuck drew his own weapon, and both began dropping Ovions at every shot. One

beam sliced the Cylon centurion's helmet in two. Only Seetol and the queen, still clutching Boxey, remained. Seetol stepped in front of Lotay to protect her.

"I want to kill them both," Starbuck said.

"Stop, Starbuck!" Apollo shouted. "You might hit Boxey."

Then Seetol sprang at Starbuck, trying to grab his weapon, which fired accidentally. A high-pitched scream ended in a gurgle as Lotay fell, head half-severed from its neck by the chance shot. Seetol's scream took up where Lotay's left off and she leaped toward the queen. Starbuck, wanting to protect Boxey, wounded Seetol in the arm with another shot. But Boxey already had struggled free of the dying queen. Sobbing wildly, he clutched the remains of Muffit to him.

Queen Lotay was dead. As in all deaths of Ovion queens, the tiny sharp points on the skin of her body faded to a dull yellow. Without her queen, Seetol had no function. She could not stop her misery. She could only sit and let life drain away from the wound in her arm.

They released Cassiopeia and the others from the pods. All followed as they searched for an elevator to take them to the surface. More Cylons appeared, and the shooting resumed. Suddenly they saw with horror that all this shooting had set fire to the Tylium. The walls of the mine were beginning to heat up and glow.

By sheer luck they found their way to the elevator. And then, as by magic, its doors opened and Boomer stepped out, smiling. "Hi, guys. What's going on? Been looking everywhere for you." He joined them in firing at Cylons and covering the retreat of the others into the elevator.

On the podium in the main hall Uri had reached the climax of his speech while the crowd cheered him: "So join with me in the spirit of the great communion and put your faith in me and go to the Cylons. You'll remember this as the foundation on which the floor of peace is—"

Then Apollo, Starbuck and Boomer raced in. Everyone gasped and stared as Apollo pointed his gun at the ceiling and fired. "This is an order. Everyone move quickly and in order to the exits."

"Stay where you are!" Uri shouted. "I'm in charge here."

Suddenly a group of Cylons burst in and began firing.

"Listen to Apollo!" Uri yelled as he ducked for cover. "Do what he says. He's in charge."

"Apollo! Boxey!" Serina ran to them. "I've been looking for you everywhere. Where are all the members of Blue Squadron who were supposed to get medals? They never showed up."

"Don't know," Apollo said, firing at Cylons. "But sure could use 'em now. Get down, Serina—Boxey. Make your way out to the garden. We'll cover you."

Over the garden a landram hovered with fat Lieutenant Jolly mounted on a gun turret. Other landrams were coming in and hovering while their guns fired at Cylons.

"Where in all that's holy did you come from, Jolly?" Apollo shouted up to him.

"Captain, we're here courtesy of Commander Adama. He sent the landrams to cover for you guys in case fighting broke out. Smartest man who ever lived, your father. He told us to collect Red Squadron and shuttle them back to *Galactica*. He's expecting a fight up there."

"Why just Red?" Apollo asked. "What about Blue Squadron?"

Jolly grinned. "At the last minute he wouldn't let Blue go to the party. Except for you, Starbuck and Boomer. Wanted you-all to play hero so Uri wouldn't get wise to his keeping the rest of us on alert on the battlestar."

"Hurry it up!" Apollo shouted. "Go, go, go! Civilians to the shuttles! When that Tylium heating up down below finally blows there's not going to be much left of this-here planet. Boxey—Serina, I'll see you later on *Galactica*!"

On the bridge of the battlestar Athena exclaimed, "Father! A full squadron is answering General Quarters. There aren't that many pilots left on board."

"Yes there are." Adama smiled grimly. "Sorry, Ensign, but I had to keep it a secret from just about everybody. And Red Squadron is on its way up here now to join them."

Nothing seemed more important than every possible pilot be on hand to meet the Cylon attack that Adama knew would come at any minute. Yet one other thing was of equal importance. In these last crucial hours, during all the chaos down on the surface, he and Tigh had been able to get enough additional food and Tylium up from Carillon to supply the entire fleet for a very long voyage. *To wherever* was the way Adama put it.

As the defense wing was revealed on the main console screen, Adama was struck by how pitifully small it looked against the wall of the advancing Cylon armada. A lead Cylon ship rolled and fired as it flew by a Viper. The Viper took the hit full on and exploded. At almost the same moment two more Vipers were destroyed.

Adama shook his head and drove his right fist into the palm of his left hand.

At last Athena called, "Red Squadron ready, Commander."

"Launch it," Adama said. "Launch everything we've got." He wished he were young enough to be going up there with Apollo, Boomer, Starbuck.

Starbuck joined the battle by wiping out four Cylon ships which had Boomer caught in a pinwheel attack. "Anybody want to fly over and touch me for luck?" he cried.

"Starbuck," Apollo said.

"Yo?"

"On your tail!"

Glancing over his shoulder, Starbuck saw a Cylon fighter coming in from each side. "Nothing to worry about," he said. But a Cylon laser torpedo came too close and the explosion sent Starbuck's ship rocking. He banked it over and away from the pair of Cylons, who continued pursuit.

"Boomer," Apollo said, "you give him a hand."

"Again? Well, I'm trying." Boomer swung over and began firing.

"Don't take too long, Boomer," Starbuck said.

Another explosion shook Starbuck's ship. Boomer got the attacker in his sights, and the Cylon fighter made a thousand beautiful little pieces.

"C'mon, Starbuck, Boomer!" Apollo yelled. "Let's triple-team 'em."

The three fighters quickly formed a triangular formation like the one they'd used in blazing a path through the mine-field. They swept together on the wall of Cylon ships, blasting left and right, up and down. Cracks formed in the Cylon ranks. A series of explosions joined many of the close-flying craft. Apollo, Starbuck and Boomer all together went into a tight turn and fled the counterattack.

———————

A bridge screen displayed huge fires on the surface of Carillon. Another screen showed the planet rocked by explosion after explosion. Nearly every human had been able to escape. Even Uri, who was said to be hiding himself somewhere on *Rising Star*.

There was a new crisis for Adama on *Galactica.* The Cylon attack had been beaten off, but now it had regrouped and was returning. Meanwhile, intelligence reported that the distant weaker portion of the fleet was about to come under attack. Furthermore, the growing intensity of the fires on Carillon showed that the entire planet might blow up and take *Galactica* and her sister ships with it.

Adama acted quickly. He sent Apollo's squadron blasting away at the new attack while the group made preparations for the hyperspace jump. The timing had to be exact—and it was. As Apollo's squadron returned to *Galactica*, the first pre-jump mechanisms were set. After the returning pilots were safely strapped in gee-couches, the jump was made.

A long moment passed, then suddenly *Galactica* found itself in the midst of the Cylon attack on the rest of the fleet. The squadron fighters raced into their ships and were catapulted into the battle. The Cylons, so adept at ambush themselves, were taken completely by surprise.

Imperious Leader was shocked by the defeat of both his Cylon task forces at the hands of the small group of human fighters. It pained him especially the way his ships had fallen prey to the diversionary action of Captain Apollo and his men. The whole campaign might have been saved except for the brilliance of those two men, Adama and Apollo. The universe must become rid of those two. And he was the one who would do it.

Previous Cylon leaders never had been so taken up with personal revenge. Imperious Leader knew that. Yet he was determined to destroy both Apollo and Adama personally. He would follow them to the ends of the universe to accomplish it. He knew that his desire for revenge was quite humanlike. Perhaps his final defeat was that he had become like his enemy. Well, so be it. He would destroy what had become human within him by destroying the humans themselves. Adama, he would kill personally. But for now he must wait.

————

Adama raised his goblet to signal a toast. Everyone around the central table at the banquet on *Galactica* grew quiet. He said, "I toast our victories and the achievement of our first goals."

"Hear, hear," said Antonie, the woman who had become the new chief of the Council. "And now I propose a toast. To Adama and the fine men and women who have fought with him to preserve our freedom. I have an announcement. I'm stepping aside as chief of Council to restore Adama to his post."

"But I've resigned," Adama told Antonie.

"But I tore up your resignation," she said. "We need you, Adama. Ladies and gentlemen, I toast hope."

Serina, seated a few places away from Adama at the center table, leaned toward him and said, "You really *do* believe we can find this place Earth, don't you, Commander?"

"Yes, I do. You may think it a dream, Serina. But sometimes dreams are worth the chasing. Along the way, who can say what we may find, what we may learn? Right now, it's a time for joy."

"I'm all for that," Starbuck said.

"Hey Starbuck," Boomer called, "when are you going to pay me off for saving your life out there?"

"As soon as you pay me off for saving yours," Starbuck replied.

Serina turned to Apollo and said, "There's only one thing prevents this from being the happiest moment of my life."

"What's that?"

"Boxey. He's still sad about losing Muffit Two."

Apollo clapped a hand to his brow and said, "I forgot! Where is our great technician? Where's Boxey?" Both appeared. The technician opened a box and out hopped a new Muffit into the arms of Boxey. It was hard to tell whether the barking droid or the laughing boy sounded happier.

Serina leaned over and kissed Apollo while all cheered. Then she raised her glass and addressed Commander Adama.

"To Earth," she said.

————